MORE
TRUE
LIES

18 TALES FOR YOU TO JUDGE

Told by
George Shannon

Illustrated by
John O'Brien

Greenwillow Books
An Imprint of HarperCollinsPublishers

Library of Congress Cataloging-in-Publication Data
More true lies : 18 tales for you to judge / told by
George Shannon ; pictures by John O'Brien.
    p.   cm.
Includes bibliographical references.
"Greenwillow Books."
Summary: Presents a collection of eighteen brief folk-
tales in which the reader is asked to explain how the
folk character lied and told the truth at the same time.
ISBN 0-688-17643-7 (trade)
ISBN 0-06-029188-5 (lib. bdg.)
1. Tales. [1. Folklore. 2. Literary recreations.]
I. O'Brien, John, (date) ill. II. Title.
PZ8.1.S49 Tr 2001   398.2   99-052860

10 9 8 7 6 5 4 3 2

For
Margaret Read MacDonald
—G. S.

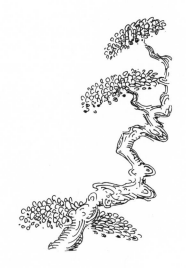

For Tess,
who is also Terase
—J. O'B.

CONTENTS

INTRODUCTION

Dictionaries give us the definitions of words, but their meanings can still be confusing. Anyone who has been tricked by another's words or has tried to avoid telling the truth while not directly lying knows that the meanings of words can be twisted. Words with more than one definition can be used purposely to confuse or to distract others from seeing the whole truth. Simply leaving out a word or two in a sentence can make the difference between telling the truth and telling the whole truth and nothing but the truth. When the goal is to deceive, there are many ways in which words can be used so that a statement is technically truthful yet basically a lie.

The following tales from around the world are retold so that you can test your skills at finding the truth in what sounds like a lie, and finding the lie in what sounds like the truth. Read carefully to discover what words these folk characters may have left out or twisted in order to mislead. And always question what the speaker's purpose might be. Is it honesty or deception?

1

STOLEN ROPE

A man in Trinidad was being led through town on his way to jail. His hands were chained behind his back, and one of his ankles was chained to the officer who was leading him. As the two men neared the village square, a former neighbor of the arrested man passed by.

"What have you done that you're in chains and sentenced to jail?"

The chained man sighed. "I picked up a rope I found on the ground."

"You poor man!" said the neighbor. "There's more injustice in the courts than I realized."

"I know. It's terrible. Please tell them to set me free."

The man being taken to jail had spoken the truth, but he was also far from innocent.

**What's the truth, the whole truth?
And where's the lie?**

⚜ THE WHOLE TRUTH

While it was true that the thief was being punished for
picking up a rope, he was lying by what he did *not* say.
The rope he picked up was tied to a cow.

2

THE COOKIE JAR

Helen's mother had just finished baking a batch of cookies when a neighbor came over and asked for help.

"I'll just be gone a few minutes," said her mother as she put the cookies into the cookie jar. "No snacking while I'm next door. These are for the party tonight."

When Helen's mother returned and checked the
cookie jar, there was only one cookie left.

"Helen!" she called as she stomped upstairs. "I told you
not to eat those cookies I made for the party tonight."

"I didn't touch one," said Helen.

"Well, they sure didn't fly away on their own! You can
stay in your room till you decide to tell the truth."

"I did tell the truth," said Helen. "I didn't touch one."

What's the truth, the whole truth?
And where's the lie?

✤| THE WHOLE TRUTH

Helen's exact words, "I didn't touch one," were true.
She had not touched *one* cookie, the only one
she'd left in the jar uneaten. She had, however,
touched—and eaten—all the rest.

3

SCHOOL DAYS

A boy came running into the house for a snack after school and gave his mother a hug.

"How was your day?" asked his mother.

The boy grinned. "I got a hundred on my math and history tests!"

"That's wonderful," said his mother. "We'll celebrate with a special supper tonight."

It was a delicious meal, but when report cards came the next week, the boy's mother discovered there had been nothing to celebrate after all.

"How could you get an F in history and a D in math when you didn't miss anything on your tests last week? Did they catch you cheating? I certainly hope you weren't telling me lies!"

"Oh, no," answered the boy. "I'd never cheat. And as sure as I didn't cheat, I told you the truth."

His mother grumbled and frowned. "Well, something's not what it seems to be. I'm sure of that."

**What's the truth, the whole truth?
And where's the lie?**

❧| THE WHOLE TRUTH

The boy *had* gotten a hundred on his math
and history tests. But it was a combined score
of 100 for both tests—a 60 on the math test
and a 40 on the history test.

4 FOREVER
STRONG

Mulla Nasrudin applied for a job as a gardener at a famous philosopher's house.

"You're getting too old, and your hair's full of gray," said the philosopher. "I need someone younger and stronger."

"What's age?" replied Nasrudin. "I'm as strong as I was twenty years ago. I'd really like the job."

The philosopher thought for a while and finally agreed.

A few days later Nasrudin was told to move slabs of stone to the back of the garden to make a path. The slabs, however, proved too heavy for him to move. The philosopher was very upset.

"This is exactly why I wanted to hire a younger man. I'm a fool for believing your lies. I ought to take you to court."

"For what?" asked Nasrudin. "I was telling the truth."

**What's the truth, the whole truth?
And where's the lie?**

❧ THE WHOLE TRUTH

Nasrudin told the truth when he said
he was as strong as he was twenty years ago.
He'd never been strong and couldn't have
moved the stones then, either.

5

A SECRET LOVE

Traditionally, young Arab women were expected to keep their faces hidden behind a veil and to have no boyfriends before they married.

It happened, however, that one young woman had a secret boyfriend. When her parents became suspicious, they decided to take her to the Hill of Truth. At the top of the hill a chain hung down from the sky. Anyone who lied as he or she held the chain would be turned to ashes.

"Tomorrow we will hire donkeys," announced her father. "You, your mother, and I will visit the hill. If you've been meeting a secret boyfriend, you won't be able to lie any longer!"

The father was pleased to find a stable that charged a very low price for its donkeys and even included a servant to ride along and tend the donkeys.

The four travelers had just reached the base of the hill when the young woman slipped and fell off her donkey. As she fell, her veil got caught on the saddle, exposing her face. Even though the servant quickly helped her back up, she wept with embarrassment.

When they reached the hilltop, the father told her to grab the chain and demanded to know if she had a secret boyfriend.

"You, dear father, and the servant who helped me today when I fell are the only men who have seen my face or touched me."

The chain of truth left the young woman alive because she was telling the truth as well as a lie.

What's the truth, the whole truth?
And where's the lie?

✒ THE WHOLE TRUTH

Knowing her father was thrifty, she had told
her boyfriend to rent him his donkeys at a very
low price and to offer to ride with them.
She had fallen on purpose so he would
have to touch her as he helped her up.

6

FIRST TOUCH

The richest man in the village was used to getting whatever he wished. In time, what he wanted most was the beautiful wife of a poor farmer. Everyone knew the farmer and his wife were very happy, but the rich man kept trying schemes to get her to marry him instead.

One winter the rich man made a wager with the farmer.

"If you succeed at the task I give you and win the wager," explained the rich man, "you may come into my house and keep the first thing you touch with your hand. But if you fail, I get to come into your house and do the same."

The farmer was so excited at the thought of touching and keeping the rich man's treasure that he quickly accepted the wager.

With the help of many assistants, the rich man made sure the farmer failed and lost the wager.

"Our agreement remains," said the rich man with a grin. "Now I get to come to your house and keep the first thing I touch. I'll be there tonight."

When the rich man and his assistants arrived, the farmer and his wife were working in the upper loft of their tiny hut. The rich man immediately climbed up and grabbed the wife's hand.

"At last!" he exclaimed. "Just as we agreed. Your wife is mine to marry now."

"No, I'm not!" said the wife.

"We agreed," insisted the rich man. "You and your husband must stick to the rules of our wager."

"Exactly," said the farmer. "And those rules prove my wife will stay here when you leave."

The assistants could only shake their heads.

What's the truth, the whole truth?
And where's the lie?

❧| THE WHOLE TRUTH

The farmer and his wife were following the rules
of the wager. In his eagerness to touch the wife's hand
and claim her, the rich man didn't stop to
realize he'd touched the ladder first as he rushed
up to the loft. Determined to stay together, the farmer
and his wife had purposely waited in the loft so the rich
man would have to touch the ladder first.

7 TROUBLE WITH TREES

One spring Tyll Eulenspiegel needed to sell his horse in order to pay some bills. The marketplace in Frankfurt was crowded with people, but few even stopped to look at his horse. At last a thin man made an offer.

"I'll give you half your asking price," said the man, "as long as he's got no problems. I need a good-tempered and gentle horse."

"That he is," said Tyll. "Gentle as a lamb. His only fault is that he won't go over trees."

"Trees!" said the man with a laugh. "Who cares about that?"

The man paid happily and rode off on the horse. But before there'd been time for Tyll to spend a cent, the man was back and yelling with rage.

"You cheat! Gentle? No problems? I can't even get this horse to ride out of town. He refuses to cross the bridge. You lied and I want my money back."

"I told you the truth," Tyll insisted. "The money stays mine."

What's the truth, the whole truth?
And where's the lie?

⊰╢ THE WHOLE TRUTH

Tyll spoke truthfully *and* misleadingly. Saying the
horse wouldn't go over trees was a sly way of saying
the horse wouldn't go over bridges made of wood.

8

THE KNIFE

A storyteller in India loved to tell an amazing story of what had happened to him one summer.

He cut open a delicious watermelon with his knife and enjoyed a cool lunch in the shade. But before he could get everything cleaned up, he had to run into the house to check on a strange sound.

When he returned, the storyteller discovered a cow had eaten all the melon rind, and the knife was nowhere to be found.

Worried that the cow might have swallowed the knife, he quickly milked the cow. But he didn't find the knife in the milk.

So he churned the milk into butter, but he didn't find the knife in the butter. After that he melted the butter into ghee for a recipe. And when he looked at the liquid ghee, he found the knife!

Though no one ever believed his story, it truly happened.

What's the truth, the whole truth?
And where's the lie?

❧| THE WHOLE TRUTH

In his hurry to check on the noise, the storyteller
had carried the knife into the house and forgot
he'd taken it there. Later, when he looked into the bowl
of liquid ghee, he saw the knife's reflection.
It was still in the ceiling beam where he'd stuck it as he
searched for the noise. By not telling the whole truth, the
storyteller had seemed to lie.

9 THE NEW SERVANT

A man who had spent his last cent began looking for work. The first person to show any interest in hiring him was a wealthy man well known for being stingy and for tricking his workers.

"What can you do if I hire you?"

"Name it and I can do it," bragged the poor man. "I've worked every trade there is."

"And what pay do you *think* you'll deserve?"

"Not much," he answered. "Just twenty dollars a year, as long as you feed and clothe me."

It was a bargain the wealthy man couldn't refuse. He reasoned that anyone fool enough to work for such low wages could easily be tricked in other ways.

"You're hired."

The new servant moved in that evening. But the next morning, when all the other servants got up to begin their work, the new servant just stayed in bed.

At noon the wealthy man came yelling into the servants' quarters. "What makes you think you can sleep all day? Stick to our agreement, or out you'll go!"

"I *am* sticking to our agreement," said the new servant. "I've been waiting since dawn for you to follow it, too."

What's the truth, the whole truth?
And where's the lie?

❧| THE WHOLE TRUTH

The phrase "feed and clothe me" has two possible
interpretations. The wealthy man took it to mean
he was to provide the new servant with clothes
and food. The new servant, eager to be lazy and
trick his boss, meant he was to be fed and
clothed as one feeds and clothes a baby.

10

SPARROWS

A miser saw a peddler walking down the street with a dozen pheasants tied to a pole.

"Sparrows!" called the peddler. "Twelve for a dollar. Sparrows for sale."

He's a fool, thought the miser. He doesn't know
the difference between pheasants and sparrows.
A dollar for twelve pheasants is truly a bargain.
"Here's a dollar for your sparrows," he said.
"Sold," said the peddler as he scooped a dozen
sparrows out of his sack.

"This is an outrage," yelled the miser. "Twelve sparrows for a dollar is far overpriced. I won't be cheated by a fool like you. I want my pheasants. Officer, arrest this man. He's a lying thief."

The officer was quick and stern. "You must give this man what he paid for."

"I did," said the peddler. "He asked for sparrows and that's what he got."

"But he lied," insisted the miser.

The three of them argued for nearly an hour.

**What's the truth, the whole truth?
And where's the lie?**

❧| THE WHOLE TRUTH

Some people, including the miser, would say
the peddler lied when he displayed pheasants
on his pole at the same time he called,
"Sparrows for sale."
Still, everything the peddler said was the truth.
In his eagerness to take advantage of the
peddler, the miser's greed created the lie
when he thought the peddler was selling
twelve pheasants for a dollar.

11 PLENTY
OF LIES

A dark-hearted khan announced that the only man he'd allow to marry his daughter had to tell one hundred lies in a row. If anyone tried and failed, the khan could chop off his head. Many tried—royalty, soldiers, and peasants alike—but some bit of truth always slipped into their stories and they failed. Men were soon afraid to come near the palace at all.

When a shepherd arrived and asked for his turn at telling a hundred lies, the khan only laughed. The idea of a shepherd's even thinking he had a chance at marrying his daughter made the khan eager to chop off the shepherd's head.

"You deserve a chance to fail and die like everyone else," he said.

As soon as the shepherd began to speak, people were amazed. Every breath brought another lie even stranger than the one before it. Not once did even a sliver of truth creep into his stories.

"There!" announced the shepherd. "I've told one hundred lies. I'll marry your daughter tomorrow."

The khan glanced at his advisors, then laughed again. "You've failed. My advisors have carefully counted, and you told only ninety-nine lies. Prepare to die."

"I told a hundred," replied the shepherd.

"Ninety-nine," insisted the khan.

What's the truth, the whole truth?
And where's the lie?

43

◄ THE WHOLE TRUTH

The shepherd's one hundredth lie was saying
that he'd already told one hundred lies when,
in fact, he'd only told ninety-nine.

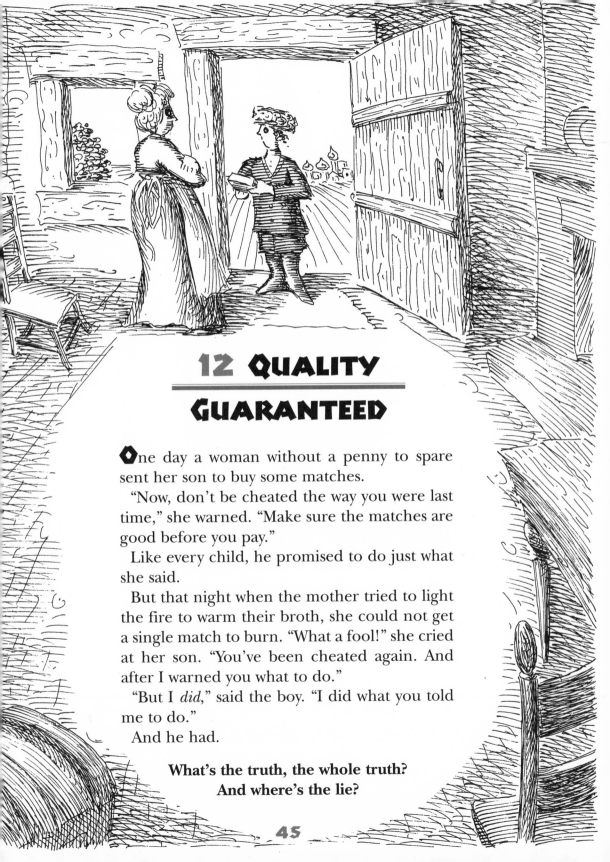

12 QUALITY
GUARANTEED

One day a woman without a penny to spare sent her son to buy some matches.

"Now, don't be cheated the way you were last time," she warned. "Make sure the matches are good before you pay."

Like every child, he promised to do just what she said.

But that night when the mother tried to light the fire to warm their broth, she could not get a single match to burn. "What a fool!" she cried at her son. "You've been cheated again. And after I warned you what to do."

"But I *did*," said the boy. "I did what you told me to do."

And he had.

**What's the truth, the whole truth?
And where's the lie?**

⚬| THE WHOLE TRUTH

The boy's mother had warned him, "Make
sure the matches are good before you pay."
He'd made sure they were good by
lighting them all before he paid.

13

WOOD FOR SALE

A poor man and his wife worked hard gathering branches and sticks to sell as firewood.

"Start with a high price," called the wife as her husband began leading their ox and wagon full of wood to town. "That way you'll have room to bargain down and still do well."

Luck brought a buyer before the woodcutter was even halfway to the village.

"How much for all that wood your ox is pulling?" called a man from the side of the road.

Remembering his wife's advice, the woodcutter asked for a high figure. It was twice the amount he expected to get, but the man agreed.

"Sold. As long as you agree to deliver it to my house a mile down the road."

The woodcutter was delighted and couldn't wait to share the good news with his wife.

"Just unhitch your ox," said the man. "You can leave the wagon and wood near the barn."

"But I can't leave my wagon," said the woodcutter.

"But *you* have no wagon to leave," said the man. "You sold it to me."

"I'd never sell my wagon!"

"You already did," said the man. "And at a very good price."

**What's the truth, the whole truth?
And where's the lie?**

🌿| THE WHOLE TRUTH

The man asked the price of "all that wood your ox is pulling." The woodcutter naturally assumed he meant just the firewood. The buyer, however, meant *all* the wood: the firewood and the wooden cart that held it.

14
MAILING GIFTS

Doris carefully wrapped her package and took it to the post office to have it weighed and mailed.

"Does it contain anything breakable?" asked the postal clerk.

"Oh, yes," said Doris.

"Then I'll stamp it FRAGILE to make sure it doesn't get dropped."

"No need to fuss with that," she said. "Dropping it won't hurt a thing."

"But I thought you said it contains something breakable?"

"It does," said Doris.

"Then I want to stamp it FRAGILE to make sure it doesn't get dropped."

"But nothing will break if you drop it."

"Please," said the postal clerk, shaking her head. "If it contains something breakable, I need to stamp it FRAGILE so it won't get dropped and break. Folks are waiting in line. I don't have time for games."

"Neither do I," insisted Doris. "I'm telling the truth." She was.

What's the truth, the whole truth?
And where's the lie?

🌿 THE WHOLE TRUTH

Doris's package contained a copy of the Bible,
which includes the Ten Commandments.
The Ten Commandments can certainly be broken.
But dropping the package would not have
caused anything to break.

15

A Tiny Hero

In ancient times on the island of Celebes a Muslim holy man was being chased by warring enemies. Fortunately he found a dark cave, crawled inside, and was saved by a spider.

"If it hadn't been for the spider," he told his friends afterward, "I surely would have been caught and killed."

The others shook their heads in disbelief. "Do you really expect us to believe that a spider saved you from a group of angry warriors?"

"It's true," said the holy man. "And from this day forward I will never harm a spider."

What's the truth, the whole truth?
And where's the lie?

❧| THE WHOLE TRUTH

The spider saved the holy man by spinning a web over
the mouth of the cave. When the enemies stopped at
the cave and saw the web, they reasoned that if
anyone had entered, the web would have
broken. Had the holy man told the whole
truth of *how* the spider helped, no one
would have thought he was telling a lie.

16 THE RIGHT PROPOSAL

As Mutanabbi, the old poet, passed Zubeida's house one day, he decided to return that evening and propose that they be married. Halfway home he met a handsome young man.

"And where are you going this beautiful day?" asked Mutanabbi.

"To see the most beautiful woman in the city," said the young man. "I'm going to ask Zubeida to marry me."

Mutanabbi was afraid Zubeida would choose the handsome young man before *he* even got a chance to propose.

"Then you should know the truth," Mutanabbi said with a sigh. "When I passed her house just moments ago, I saw her kissing a wealthy man."

Feeling he had no chance against a wealthy suitor, the young man turned around and went home.

Later, when he learned that Mutanabbi had married Zubeida, he felt betrayed.

"I can't believe her family chose you instead of the rich man," argued the young man, "unless you lied about seeing her kiss a rich man just to keep me away."

"Not at all," insisted Mutanabbi. "I saw them with my own eyes."

And he had, but it was also true he'd tricked the young man.

What's the truth, the whole truth?
And where's the lie?

❧ THE WHOLE TRUTH

Mutanabbi had seen Zubeida kissing a wealthy man.
But it was also true that the wealthy man was
her father, not another suitor.

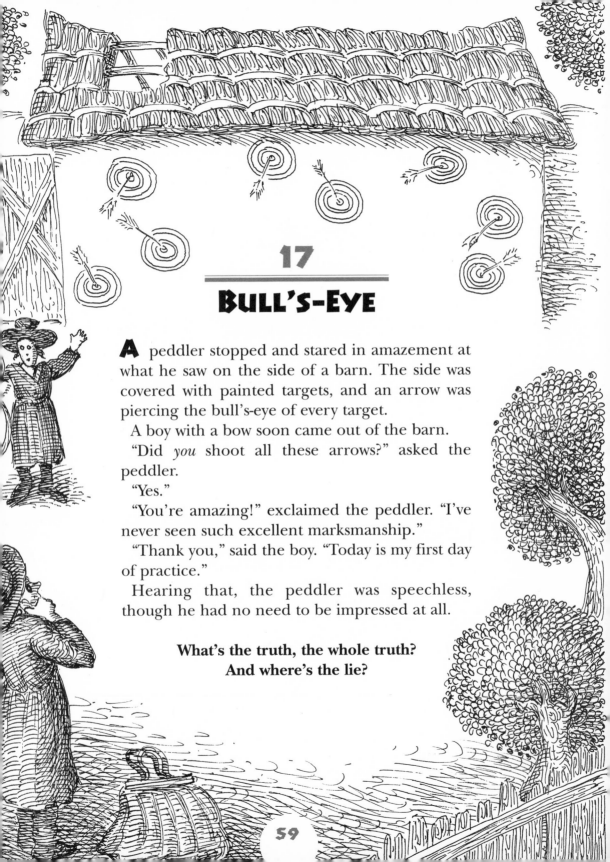

17

BULL'S-EYE

A peddler stopped and stared in amazement at what he saw on the side of a barn. The side was covered with painted targets, and an arrow was piercing the bull's-eye of every target.

A boy with a bow soon came out of the barn.

"Did *you* shoot all these arrows?" asked the peddler.

"Yes."

"You're amazing!" exclaimed the peddler. "I've never seen such excellent marksmanship."

"Thank you," said the boy. "Today is my first day of practice."

Hearing that, the peddler was speechless, though he had no need to be impressed at all.

What's the truth, the whole truth?
And where's the lie?

❧| THE WHOLE TRUTH

The boy had shot all the arrows.
But he hadn't painted the targets
until *after* the arrows had hit the barn.

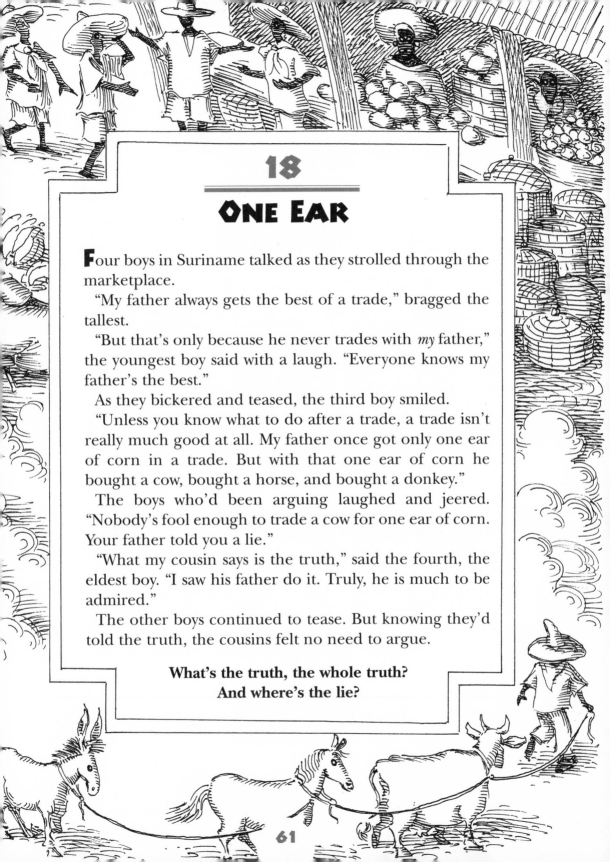

18

ONE EAR

Four boys in Suriname talked as they strolled through the marketplace.

"My father always gets the best of a trade," bragged the tallest.

"But that's only because he never trades with *my* father," the youngest boy said with a laugh. "Everyone knows my father's the best."

As they bickered and teased, the third boy smiled.

"Unless you know what to do after a trade, a trade isn't really much good at all. My father once got only one ear of corn in a trade. But with that one ear of corn he bought a cow, bought a horse, and bought a donkey."

The boys who'd been arguing laughed and jeered. "Nobody's fool enough to trade a cow for one ear of corn. Your father told you a lie."

"What my cousin says is the truth," said the fourth, the eldest boy. "I saw his father do it. Truly, he is much to be admired."

The other boys continued to tease. But knowing they'd told the truth, the cousins felt no need to argue.

What's the truth, the whole truth?
And where's the lie?

⚘ THE WHOLE TRUTH

The man did start with one ear of corn, then bought a
cow, bought a horse, and bought a donkey, but not all
at once as the laughing boys assumed. Over time, the
man planted the ear of corn. Sold the crop. Bought a
cow. Sold it and bought a horse. Sold it and bought a
donkey. Given time, things that sound impossible
can become a truth.

NOTES

1. "Stolen Rope" is adapted from "Noodle Stories—#14" in *Folk-lore of the Antilles, French and English, Part I* by Elsie Clews Parsons (New York: Memoirs of the American Folk-Lore Society, 1933). Variants can be found in *Jewish Folktales* selected and retold by Pinhas Sadeh (New York: Doubleday, 1989), *Hot Springs and Hell and Other Folk Jests and Anecdotes from the Ozarks* collected by Vance Randolph (Hatboro, PA: Folklore Associates, 1965), and "Celestial Humour: Selections from the 'Hsiao Lin Kuang' or Book of Laughter" by G. Taylor in *The China Review*, Volume 14, 1885–86.

2. "The Cookie Jar" is North American lore retold from *Barrel of Fun: A Stunt Book Chock-Full of Jokes & Riddles & Puzzles, Tricks to Try, Things to Make, Stunts to Do* selected by Edna Preston (New York: Scholastic, 1957) and *The Toastmaster's Treasure Chest* edited by Herbert V. Prochnow and Herbert V. Prochnow, Jr. (New York: Harper, 1979).

3. "School Days" is a folk anecdote found in Jordan and the United States. It is retold from *Laughing Together: Giggles and Grins from Around the Globe* compiled by Barbara K. Walker (Minneapolis: Free Spirit, 1992 [1977]), and *Great Riddles, Giggles and Jokes Written by Kids* compiled by Anna Pansini (New York: Troll, 1990).

4. "Forever Strong" is one of the countless tales told about the Middle Eastern character Mulla Nasrudin. It is retold from *The Subtleties of the Inimitable Mulla Nasrudin* by Indries Shah (New York: Dutton, 1973) and *Mulla's Donkey and Other Friends* adapted by Mehdi Nakosteen (Boulder, CO: Este Es Press/University of Colorado Libraries, 1974).

5. "A Secret Love" is adapted from a tale for adults found in *Arab Folktales* translated and edited by Inea Bushnaq (New York: Pantheon, 1986), and *Popular Tales and Fictions* by W. A. Clouston (Edinburgh: Blackwood, 1887). Variants have also been collected in China, France, Iceland, and Mexico.

6. "First Touch" is retold from *Tawi Tales: Folk Tales from Jammu* by Noriko Mayeda and W. Norman Brown (New Haven, CT: American Oriental Society, 1974) and *Bannu, or Our Afghan Frontier* by Septimus S. Thornburn (London: Trubner, 1876). A Chechen variant is in *How the Moolah Was Taught a Lesson and Other Tales from Russia* translated and adapted by Estelle Titiev and Lila Pargment (New York: Dial, 1976) and *Folk Tales from the Soviet Union* edited by The Russian Federation (Moscow: Raduga, 1986).

7. "Trouble with Trees" is one of the many tales often told about Tyll Eulenspiegel. It is retold from *Master Tyll Owlglass: His Marvellous Adventures and Rare Conceits* translated by K. R. H. MacKenzie (London: Routledge & Sons, 1923) and *Master Till's Amazing Pranks: The Story of Till Eulenspiegel* retold by Lisbeth Gombrich and Clara Hemsted (New York: Chanticleer Press, 1948). Variants have also been collected in England, Finland, Lithuania, and Hungary.

8. "The Knife" is retold from *The History of the Bene Israel of India* by Haeem Samuel Kehimkar (Tel Aviv: Dayag Press, 1937).

9. "The New Servant" is a Serbian tale retold from "The Servant Who Was Smarter Than His Master" in *Nine Magic Pea-Hens and Other Serbian Tales* collected by Vuk Karadzic, chosen and translated by John Adlard (Edinburgh: Floris, 1988). Karadzic's retellings were originally published in Europe between 1821 and 1853.

10. "Sparrows" is retold from "How Kichigo the Jester Sold Sparrows" in *The Twilight Hour: Legends, Fables and Fairy Tales from All Over the World* by Vladislav Stanovsky and Jan Vladislav, translated by Jean Layton (London: Paul Hamlyn, 1961/1966). Stanovsky identifies the tale as Japanese but gives no sources.

11. "Plenty of Lies" is retold from "A Hundred Lies" in *The Kaha Bird: Tales from the Steppes of Central Asia* translated and edited by Mirra Ginsburg (New York: Crown, 1971). Saving one's life by being able to tell skillful or outlandish lies at the right time occurs in tales around the world.

12. "Quality Guaranteed" is retold from "He Tries the Matches" in *Filled with Laughter: A Fiesta of Jewish Folk Humor* (New York: Yoseloff, 1961). Variants featuring fruit appear in *Laughing Together: Stories, Riddles and Proverbs from Asia and the Pacific* from the Asian Cultural Centre (New Delhi, India: National Book Trust, 1986) and *One Hundred Parables of Zen* translated by Joyce Lim (Singapore: Asiapac Books, 1995).

13. "Wood for Sale" is a plot found in many central and eastern Asian cultures. It is retold from "Ooka and the Barbered Beast" in *Ooka the Wise: Tales of Old Japan* by I. G. Edmonds (Indianapolis, IN: Bobbs-Merrill, 1961), and "The Best of the Bargain" in *Just One More* by Jeanne B. Hardendorff (Philadelphia: Lippincott, 1969). Hardendorff's source was *Hajji Baba of Ispahan* by James Morier (1851).

14. "Mailing Gifts" is adapted from North American joke-lore. It is retold from *The Little Joke Book* (Mt. Vernon, NY: Peter Pauper Press, 1959), *More Jokes, Jokes, Jokes* selected by Helen Hoke (New York: Franklin Watts, 1965), and *Tales from the Bagel Lancers: Everyman's Book of Jewish Humor* selected by Gerry Blumenfeld (Cleveland: World, 1967).

15. "A Tiny Hero" is a Muslim tale retold from "Pursuit of the Hadji" in *Kantchil's Lime Pit and Other Stories from Indonesia* by Harold Courlander (New York: Harcourt, 1950) and "Mohammed and the Spider" in *Indonesian Legends and Folk Tales* by Adele de Leeuw (New York: Nelson, 1961). A Jewish variant involving King David can be found in *Tales from the Wise Men of Israel* retold by Judith Ish-Kishor (Philadelphia: Lippincott, 1961). Variants have also been collected in Japan, Africa, Lapland, and India.

16. "The Right Proposal" is retold from "Mutanabbi, the Old Scholar" in *Myths and Legends of the Swahili* by Jan Knappert (London: Heinemann Educational Books, 1970).

17. "Bull's-Eye" is retold from "Hitting the Bull's Eye" in *A Treasury of Jewish Folklore* edited by Nathan Ausubel (New York: Crown, 1948) and *Braude's Treasury of Wit and Humor* by Jacob M. Braude (Englewood Cliffs, NJ: Prentice-Hall, 1964), which features an army soldier.

18. "One Ear" is adapted and retold from riddle number 20 in *Suriname Folk-Lore* collected by Melville J. Herskovits and Frances S. Herskovits (New York: AMS Press, 1969, 1936).